What Kids Say About
Carole Marsh Mysteries . . .

I love the real locations! Reading the book always makes me want to go and visit them all on our next family vacation. My Mom says maybe, but I can't wait!

One day, I want to be a real kid in one of Ms. Marsh's mystery books. I think it would be fun, and I think I am a real character anyway. I filled out the application and sent it in and am keeping my fingers crossed!

History was not my favorite subject until I starting reading Carole Marsh Mysteries. Ms. Marsh really brings history to life. Also, she leaves room for the scary and fun.

I think Christina is so smart and brave. She is lucky to be in the mystery books because she gets to go to a lot of places. I always wonder just how much of the book is true and what is made up. Trying to figure that out is fun!

Grant is cool and funny! He makes me laugh a lot!!

I like that there are boys and girls in the story of different ages. Some mysteries I outgrow, but I can always find a favorite character to identify with in these books.

They are scary, but not too scary. They are funny. I learn a lot. There is always food which makes me hungry. I feel like I am there.

What Parents and Teachers Say About Carole Marsh Mysteries . . .

I think kids love these books because they have such a wealth of detail. I know I learn a lot reading them! It's an engaging way to look at the history of any place or event. I always say I'm only going to read one chapter to the kids, but that never happens—it's always two or three, at least!
—Librarian

Reading the mystery and going on the field trip—Scavenger Hunt in hand—was the most fun our class ever had! It really brought the place and its history to life. They loved the real kids characters and all the humor. I loved seeing them learn that reading is an experience to enjoy! —4th grade teacher

Carole Marsh is really on to something with these unique mysteries. They are so clever; kids want to read them all. The Teacher's Guides are chock full of activities, recipes, and additional fascinating information. My kids thought I was an expert on the subject—and with this tool, I felt like it!
—3rd grade teacher

My students loved writing their own mystery book!
Ms. Marsh's reproducible guidelines are a real jewel. They learned about copyright and ended up with their own book they were so proud of!
—Reading/Writing Teacher

"The kids seem very realistic—my children seemed to relate to the characters. Also, it is educational by expanding their knowledge about the famous places in the books."

"They are what children like: mysteries and adventures with children they can relate to."

"Encourages reading for pleasure."

"This series is great. It can be used for reluctant readers, and as a history supplement."

MASTERS OF DISASTERS

By
Carole Marsh

Published by Gallopade International/Carole Marsh Books. Printed in the
United States of America.

Managing Editor: Sherry Moss
Senior Editor: Janice Baker
Assistant Editor: Mike Kelly
Cover Design & Illustrations: John Kovaleski (www.kovaleski.com)
Content Design: Darryl Lilly, Outreach Graphics

Gallopade International is introducing SAT words that kids need to know
in each new book that we publish. The SAT words are bold in the story.
Look for this special logo beside each word in the glossary. Happy Learning!

Gallopade is proud to be a member and supporter of these educational
organizations and associations:

American Booksellers Association

American Library Association

International Reading Association

National Association for Gifted Children

The National School Supply and Equipment Association

The National Council for the Social Studies

Museum Store Association

Association of Partners for Public Lands

Association of Booksellers for Children

Note from the Author

Once, I went on a trip to the Greek islands. It was night when our plane landed on the island of Santorini. We went down many steps to get to our room in an inn. When I woke up the next morning, I discovered that we had spent the night in the crater (caldera) of an ancient volcano! Fortunately, the volcano was dormant—I think!

I once read of a couple who spent all their married life as volcanologists—scientists who study volcanoes. One day, after visiting most of the world's famous volcanoes (even during eruptions!), they were standing on some hot lava when the black crust broke through and they both fell to their fiery death. Sounds bad, doesn't it? But people who knew them said they died doing something that they loved and they were well aware of the risks of researching volcanoes.

Perhaps your parents recall when Mount St. Helens erupted. Most people think volcanoes are extinct or dormant, but that is not always true. For many years, scientists had looked to find the volcano inside Yellowstone National Park. Recently, a photo made from space showed that the volcano is so big that it is not inside Yellowstone—Yellowstone is inside it! WOW!

I hope you enjoy this book on such a "hot" topic! Maybe you should read it while standing in a cool pool!

Carole Marsh

Christina   Mimi   Papa   Grant

Hey, kids! As you see, here we are ready to embark on another of our exciting Carole Marsh Mystery adventures. My grandchildren often travel with me all over the world as I research new books. We have a great time together, and learn things we will carry with us for the rest of our lives!

I hope you will go to www.carolemarshmysteries.com and explore the many Carole Marsh Mysteries series!

Well, the *Mystery Girl* is all tuned up and ready for "take-off!" Gotta go...Papa says so! Wonder what I've forgotten this time?

Happy "Armchair Travel" Reading,

Mimi

About the Characters

Artemis Masters is an absentminded genius. He's a scientist at the top of his field in the early detection of natural disasters. Everyone looks to him to solve the mysteries of nature…he just needs someone to find his car keys, shoes and glasses!

Curie Masters, though only 11, has inherited her father's intelligence and ability to see things others don't. She has a natural penchant to solve mysteries…even if it means tangling with those older and supposedly smarter than her.

Nick Masters, an 8-year-old boy who's tall enough to pass as 12, likes to match wits with his sister and has her desire to solve mysteries others overlook. While he's the younger sibling, he tends to want to protect his sister, and of course, be the first to solve the mystery.

Books in this Series:

Table of Contents

CHAPTER ONE:

That's One Hot Robot!

"Run the problem-solving software," Curie Masters said.

"Check," Copernicus Masters replied. "HR's systems are A-OK."

"Roger that," Curie said. "Turn on HR's power source."

Curie gazed at the monitor, as her younger brother removed the access key from his pocket and opened the power source access panel at HR's back. Trying to open the panel without the key, which had a special access code, would turn on a self-destruct system.

"Check," Copernicus (who preferred to be called "Nick") said, as he punched a ten-digit code on a numbered keypad inside the panel. It allowed him access to HR's main computer and power source. Nothing happened! "Curie, I forgot the code. What is it again?"

Brothers! Curie thought. "I would think you could remember a simple set of numbers," she said.

"Hey, I can't remember everything," Nick said. "Besides, you're eleven, and you still forget that I'm only eight, because I'm just about as tall as you!"

Curie knew there was no point in arguing. "Okay," she said. "The code is—1, Charlie, Alpha, Romeo, 9, Oscar, Lima, Echo, 7,9," she said, using the NATO Phonetic Alphabet to indicate 1CAR9OLE79. As Nick punched in the last number, a slight hissing sound escaped from the bay door when it snapped open. "Turning on HR's power source," he said, flipping up a switch.

Curie scanned the power indicator on another computer's monitor. "Roger that, we have power."

Nick closed the bay door, locked the access panel, and rushed to their Masters of Disasters van. Antennae stuck out at various angles on the van's exterior, making it look like a Martian extraterrestrial vehicle.

He leaped through the side door of the van and let it slam shut behind him. "Mission accomplished! HR's power source is hot," Nick said, stuffing himself into his cushioned chair in front of a bay of computer monitors.

"I know! I watched you, remember?" Curie asked, gazing at the largest monitor before her. HR stood motionless as he waited for the command that would spark his circuits to life.

"Nick," Curie said "what took you so long?"

"When you're working around delicate equipment and the most advanced motion computer chip in the world, you have to take your time so you don't make any mistakes," Nick replied.

Dr. Artemis Masters, the children's father, sat at his control panel at the front of the van. As a scientist, his specialty was the detection of natural disasters. He looked a lot like a mad scientist, with a wild mop of bright red hair that covered just the back and sides of his head. An oversized white lab coat hung on his bony shoulders and a pair of glasses balanced **precariously** on the end of his nose, while another pair swayed back and forth from a chain around his neck.

"Isn't that right, Dad?" Nick asked.

Artemis was deep in thought. He had a knack for focusing on the problem at hand and blocking out everything else around him, so it took a few seconds for his son's question to penetrate his subconscious mind. "Ahh, yes, Nick, that's right. One can never be too careful."

Dr. Suni Ki sat to the side of Artemis. Suni was Artemis' main contact at the International Association of Volcanology, or IAV, the group paying for Artemis' current project. She was also a volcanologist at Hawaii's Mauna Loa volcano.

"You two amaze me," Suni said. "I can't find my way around computers. In fact, I can't stand to work with them. But to you guys, it's second nature."

"Yeah," Nick said. "A lot of things come naturally to us."

"Please don't compliment him," Curie said, "or I'll have to put up with his ego the rest of the trip."

Suni ran her fingers over her mouth, like she was zipping a zipper. "I'll keep my mouth shut," she promised.

Artemis stood up and moved next to the children. He pressed a microphone close to his mouth, ready to record this test run for later analysis. "This is the final laboratory test of HR," he said.

HR, which stood for Humanlike Robot, had been designed to imitate the movements of the human body. He was meant to take the place of researchers in situations where it was too risky to send a real person, such as the interior of an active volcano crater.

Artemis believed that he finally got the software and mechanics right with the help of his two young, but extremely intelligent, children. Nick was named after Nicolaus Copernicus, the first person to propose that the sun is the center of the universe. Curie got her name from Marie Curie, who was famous for her work on radioactivity and a two-time Nobel Prize winner.

Artemis turned toward Curie. "Turn on the wireless transmitter," he said, wiping a thin layer of sweat from his brow.

"You sure you know how to do that?" Nick asked.

"Very funny, Nick," Curie said, as her hands flew across the keyboard in front of her. "Check. System is transmitting a signal." She gazed at the image on the monitor, which showed a secluded area of Yellowstone National Park.

Suni's group of volcanologists had hired a movie special effects company to transform the area into the barren landscape surrounding the caldera, or crater, of a volcano. It was an exact copy of a small portion of the rim of Hawaii's Mauna Loa volcano. This was where HR would have his first active field test if today's test went well.

"Power up and turn on the heat shield system," Artemis said.

Artemis had designed HR's outer skin to withstand the high temperatures found in the interior of a volcano. The combination of different metals and non-metal materials made it almost indestructible.

"Do you think you can remember the code without my help?" Curie asked.

Nick stuck his tongue out at his sister, as he punched in the code.

"Heat shield system is on line," Nick muttered.

Nick leaned back in his chair as he monitored the instruments in front of him. They would point out any problems HR might be having.

"Everything is A-OK," Nick said. "We are ready to go."

"Okay! Let's do..." Artemis started to say. He suddenly stopped and walked to the front of the van, picked up a pad of paper with calculations on it and walked back. He stood there quietly for a minute. "What were we about to do?" he asked.

"Turn on HR," Nick said.

"Oh yes," Artemis said. "Turn on HR."

"Check," Curie said, typing in another code.

HR lurched to life. The lens covers over his camera eyes flittered open. He turned his head back and forth a few times, scanning the area around him. Although he couldn't see them inside the van, HR's computer told him that Curie and Nick were online with him.

"Good morning, Miss Curie," HR said. "It's good to see you again. How are you?"

"I'm doing great, HR," Curie replied.

"And you, Mr. Nick?" HR asked.

"I couldn't be better, unless I was sitting on the beach in Hawaii," Nick answered, as his eyes flew over the readouts on his monitor. "I have to say, you look very good today, HR."

"I feel very well, thank you," HR replied. "Is Mr. Masters with you today?" he asked.

Curie moved him forward with a touch of the joystick mounted to her keyboard. For the lab tests, she controlled HR's movements. During the field tests, his automated motion system would be activated, and he would control his own movements.

Artemis was happy to see how easily HR moved. Controlling his balance, standing, twisting, walking, and bending his arms, wrists, and fingers had been major challenges.

Any robot built to descend into the fiery pits of a volcano must be able to control its own movements. When it saw an obstacle, it needed to know instantly how to handle it.

Curie and Nick had helped Artemis design HR's motion computer chip. It could analyze over a million bits of information per second, which was nothing compared to other chips on the market. But what made it different was that the information stored on

the chip allowed incredible humanlike movements in HR's arms and legs.

"Mr. Masters, are you having a good day?" HR asked.

"Yes, HR," Artemis said. "It's a good day. Are you ready for today's test?"

"I will perform my duties as required," HR answered.

Artemis turned and looked at Dr. Suni Ki. This test needed to go well today to impress her. "I sure hope so," Artemis muttered nervously under his breath.

CHAPTER TWO

Cooking with Gas

With a few twists, turns, and flicks of the joystick, Curie brought HR back over the rim of the fake, but very realistic volcano. He was covered in volcanic ash and soot, but had performed flawlessly. "Operating limits are normal," Nick said. "Dad, I think this test **validates** all the previous tests. HR is ready for field testing."

"Yes, he is," Artemis said, with a sigh of relief. Suni would be able to report back to her IAV partners that HR was on track. It wouldn't be long before HR was changing the way scientists looked at volcanoes.

"How did I do, Mr. Masters?" HR asked.

"You were great, HR," Artemis said, knowing he was talking to a set of pre-recorded phrases that HR's CPU sorted through for use in the right situations.

"Thanks for all your hard work, HR," Artemis said.

"You are welcome, Mr. Masters," HR said. "I am looking forward to our next tests."

"Curie, you can shut HR down now," Artemis said. "Nick, give HR a good bath before you put him away."

"Okay, Dad," Nick said, yanking HR's power source panel access key from his pocket. "What should I do with this?" he said, holding the key up for his dad to see.

"Leave it on the desk. I'll take care of it," Artemis said.

"Okay," Nick said, setting the panel access key down next to the van's entry door key.

Dr. Suni Ki stood up. "Impressive, Artemis. Very impressive," she said. "In fact, I have never seen anything like it before. HR moves with the grace of a ballet dancer, but has the strength of an Olympic weight lifter."

Artemis let out another sigh. "I'm glad you liked what you saw," he said. "But I'm sure that once he gets down into a live volcano, you will be even more impressed."

"I'm sure I will," Suni agreed, stepping to the van's door. "I'll let the other association members know how far along you have come. Are you sure we can't have HR transported to Hawaii for you?"

"Thanks, but I've already made the arrangements to get him over there," Artemis replied.

Suni nodded her head. "Okay, then. I will see all of you in a couple of days."

"Kids, I'm sorry about ruining another summer vacation for you," Artemis said, turning toward the children. "I know you just wanted to lay around, read, play video games, and chill, as you say."

"Dad," Curie said, "you're not ruining our vacation. We love helping you on your projects. Isn't that right, Nick?"

Nick nodded, as he rolled some data cable onto a wooden spool. "Wouldn't have it any other way. Besides, how many kids get to help build a robot and go to Hawaii over the summer?"

"Thanks, guys," Artemis said. "I'll tell you what. As soon as I finish up some final calculations, we'll go down to see Yellowstone's famous geysers and hot springs. Our flight to Hawaii leaves in four days, so we have some time to play."

"All right!" Nick said. "Now we're cooking with gas!"

"We are?" Curie asked, looking around for a fire. "Where?"

"Come on, Curie," Nick said. "You're supposed to be the smart one. I heard Grandpa say that phrase once. It means that everything is going well or that whatever you want to happen is going to happen."

"I may be the older one," Curie said, "but I don't come up with outdated expressions. Why not just say, 'Awesome'?"

"That'll work, too," Nick said, hopping from the van to the pavement. As he turned, he saw a bearded man watching him from a car across the street. A second man sat next to him, but Nick couldn't see his face. When their eyes met, the bearded man yanked something from his ear, started the car, and drove off.

Now, that was weird, Nick thought.

CHAPTER THREE:

Yellowstone Rocks!

Artemis jumped out of the van first and saw the crowds around Old Faithful, a sure indication that the geyser was about to erupt. "Come on, kids," he called. "It's going to blow any minute!" He ran toward the geyser, his white lab coat flying behind him.

"What's taking you so long?" Nick said in a mock voice, repeating what Curie had said to him earlier.

As she passed by the desk, Curie noticed that HR's panel access key was still lying there. "Dad forgot to take the key," she said.

"So take it and let's get going, or we'll have to wait around for the next eruption," Nick said.

Curie quickly hung the key on the gold chain she wore around her neck and ran out the door behind Nick.

They made it to Old Faithful just in time. "Wow!" Curie said, as they watched a steaming hot column of water shoot skyward. "How high do you think that is, Dad?"

"If I remember right," Artemis said, "Old Faithful can shoot a tower of scalding hot water more than 100 feet into the air for a minute and a half up to five minutes."

"This is so cool!" Curie shouted, clapping her hands.

"Technically it's not," Nick remarked. "After all, it is scalding hot water." Nick snapped his fingers. "That's it! Every visitor

should get a lobster on a stick, and we could hold them out over the boiling hot geyser to cook them!"

Artemis turned toward his son. "You don't impress easily, do you, Nick?" Artemis said, absentmindedly trying to place the glasses around his neck on top of the ones perched on his nose. "What if I told you that Yellowstone was the world's first national park and that it covers an area of close to 3,500 square miles and has 290 waterfalls?"

Nick yawned, stretching his arms out to his sides.

"Okay," Artemis said, "how about the fact that there are wild buffalo and two different kinds of bears living here?"

Nick looked slightly more interested.

"Or that there are approximately 2,000 earthquakes every year," Artemis continued, "and that Yellowstone is considered an active volcano because of its hot steam vents and geysers? In fact, there are over 10,000 thermal features in the park."

Nick stood up a little straighter, and his ears seemed to poke forward.

"Yellowstone is one of only three known super volcanoes," Artemis explained. "Four miles beneath the park's surface is a 40-mile-wide chamber full of molten rock that is under incredible pressure. It powers all of the park's fantastic geysers, hot springs, mud pots, and fumaroles, or vents where steam and hot sulfur dioxide gases are emitted."

"What are mud pots?" Nick asked.

Artemis could see that Nick was finally getting interested.

"They're turbulent pools of hot, muddy water that can form weird landscapes," Artemis said. "It's like watching pudding boil."

"Cool," Nick said.

"No, it's hot," Curie said, giggling.

"Yellowstone's 45-by-30 mile crater is so big," Artemis said, talking in a deeper voice, "that it took NASA to identify it from space. Some people believe that Yellowstone is due to erupt again. If it did, it would throw so much ash and gases into the sky that it would dampen the sunlight for many years, cooling the earth drastically, which would kill an incredible amount of plant and animal life. Life as we know it would change forever."

"Awesome," Nick said. "See, now I can see how Yellowstone rocks! That's the kind of information you should have told me to begin with. When can we go see the mud..."

"Artemis! Is that you?" A tall, thin man interrupted Nick.

Artemis turned toward the voice. "Bob! Bob Connors!" he said. "It's been years since..."

"College!" Bob said. "I can't believe I've stumbled into you." He saw Nick fidgeting out of the corner of his eye. "I'm sorry to interrupt. I just can't believe that after all these years..."

"That's okay," Nick said. "Dad, can Curie and I go for a hike through the hot springs?"

"Sure," Artemis said, looking at his watch. "Let's meet back at the van in an hour."

"Last one there is a sloppy mud pot," Curie said, as she and her brother raced toward the hot springs.

CHAPTER FOUR:

Bubble, Bubble, Toil and Trouble

Nick quickly took the lead. Curie and Nick were competitive in everything they did, but more so with each other. Curie struggled to catch Nick. As they approached the trail, Nick stumbled on a tree root, and Curie closed the gap between them. "I'm on your tail, little brother," she shouted. She was an arm's length from his back.

Nick ran around a massive tree and onto the beginning of the trail. "Too late," Nick shouted, as he jumped up and down like a football player who'd just scored a touchdown. He stopped jumping when he saw Curie staring at something behind him. As he turned, he couldn't believe his eyes. A misty fog floated over the hot springs. The sunlight radiating through the fog fractured into thin beams of light, creating dazzling colors and reflections on the water's surface.

"That's awesome," Nick said.

"It's beautiful," Curie added. "I wish Dad was with us."

Nick saw a bridge over the springs to his right. "Come on," he said. "There's a bridge, and the sign says it leads to the mud pots. We've got to see the bubbling mud."

They crossed the bridge and approached the mud pots. "It does look like boiling pudding," Curie observed, "just like Dad said."

"Yeah, but he forgot to mention how much they smell like rotten eggs," Nick replied. "But, they sure do bubble a lot."

"That's the sulfur coming up through vents," Curie said. "The mud pots are close to one of the major vents that the lava originally flowed through after the crater collapsed."

Nick picked up a handful of stones and sauntered onto another bridge that led to a mountain-hiking trail. He stopped in the middle of the bridge. "I wonder if you can skip stones on the surface of this stuff," he said, reaching his arm back to fling a flat stone across the boiling muddy surface. Suddenly, he stopped.

He was facing the bridge entrance. The bearded man he saw in the car earlier in the day was now there, blocking the bridge. Nick didn't like the look on his face. "Come on, Curie!" he said. "We have to go!"

"Why?" Curie asked. "What's the rush?

Nick grabbed her hand and spun her toward the other end of the bridge. Now there was another man standing there! "Just stay close to me!" he cried.

Nick ran toward the man at the far end of the bridge. The man put his arms out, like a football player about to tackle the quarterback. Nick looked over his shoulder and saw the bearded man running after them.

So it's not my imagination, he thought. He flung his handful of rocks at the man's face. They peppered his forehead and face. The man grabbed for his eyes and stumbled backward. Nick pushed his sister around the man's side onto solid ground. The man's eyes were closed, but he threw his arms out trying to catch them. He was between Nick and Curie.

As the bearded man closed in on them, Nick pushed the first man into the bearded man. They crashed into each other.

"Let's go!" Nick shouted, grabbing his sister's hand again. They raced up the trail into a grove of tall trees. As they ran uphill,

Nick scanned the area behind them. The two men were still struggling to get up without tumbling into the hot mud.

After a minute, Curie stumbled to a stop. She was panting heavily from the uphill run. "What was that about?" she wheezed.

"I'm not sure," Nick said, as he told her about the bearded man he'd seen earlier in the day.

"You don't think Dad might have a security detail assigned to us, do you?" Curie asked.

"Naw!" Nick said, pulling her further up the trail. "Besides, if they were security they would have said so." Nick ran his skinny fingers over his chin. "No, those guys were a little overly **zealous** to be security guys. I don't know what yet. But we'll figure it out."

"I wonder what they want," Curie muttered. "Maybe they want to steal HR!"

"HR's of no use to them unless they plan on using him to fetch them a boiling hot cup of coffee," Nick said, staring at Curie. "Besides, why try to kidnap us when HR is sitting all by himself in the van?"

The kids came across a small clearing in the the center of the grove of trees. Curie's eyes widened and she froze.

RROOOAARRR!

"What now?" Nick said, as he turned toward the noise.

CHAPTER FIVE:

Itty, Bitty, Little Bear

A baby black bear cub galloped toward them. He plopped at their feet and rolled back and forth playfully. Nick bent down to pet him and rubbed his tummy. "Don't do that, Nick!" Curie said. "He may bite you."

"He's just a baby cub," Nick said. "He isn't going to hurt anyone. Are you, you itty bitty little bear?"

Curie, not wanting to be bested by her brother, bent down and stroked the cub's shiny black fur. "Don't be **stingy**," she said. "Let me pet him, too." The bear rolled around and playfully nibbled at their hands.

"He's just like a puppy or a kitten," Nick said. "I guess babies are the same, no matter what kind of animal they are."

After a minute of petting and tickling by the children, the cub sat upright. Its ears stood up straight. "Well, we'd better be going," Nick said. "This guy's mommy is probably nearby, and I'm sure she won't be as friendly as he is."

Nick heard some twigs break behind them and turned. The two men had followed them up the trail.

"There they are, McGee," the bearded man said to his partner.

Nick leaped to his feet. "Come on!" he shouted, as he yanked on Curie's arm, dragging her up the trail.

ROOOOAAAARRRR!!!

Nick and Curie froze. Looming in front of them was the biggest bear they had ever seen. The bear stood up straight and stretched its massive arms. Razor-sharp claws stuck out of each paw. Its mouth was larger

than Nick's whole head. He would only be a bite-sized snack for her.

"Sheppard, get ready to grab her," McGee said to the bearded man, as they slowly approached Nick and Curie from behind.

Nick looked at Curie. "We've got to run for it," he said.

"Are you crazy?" Curie asked.

"Hey, it's the bear or them," Nick said. "And I think we've got a better chance with the bear." He took a deep breath, and just as the bear roared and spread its paws again, he shouted, "Run!"

Nick and Curie dashed under the bear's outstretched paws and up the trail further into the woods. Sheppard, the bearded man, had leaped forward to grab them just as Nick and Curie bolted past the bear, causing the bear to think the man was going to attack her. She ignored Nick and Curie and started chasing

Sheppard and McGee through the woods. The baby cub and another little cub trailed after her.

Nick looked behind them and laughed. "Look at those babies run," he said. "And I don't mean the little cubbies!"

"Wow," Curie said, "those guys are really having a bad day."

"Hey!" Nick cried, as he started to head back down the trail. "They don't call us the Masters of Disasters for nothing!"

Nick peered at his watch through his thick glasses. Their father was going to be worried if they didn't get back quickly. Something the bearded man said replayed in Nick's mind. "Get ready to grab her!" *He suddenly realized they didn't want him—they only wanted his sister, Curie!*

CHAPTER SIX

Sounds Suspicious

"I'm sure glad you guys are okay," Artemis said, climbing into the driver's seat of the van. "Mothers of all kinds are very protective of their cubs." He scanned the cockpit-like arrangement of gauges in front of him, looking for something. He tilted the visor and then put it back up. He checked the cup holders near his right elbow and then started to pat his pockets. He finally found the keys in his front right pocket and cranked the van's engine to life.

"We were careful, Dad," Curie said, strapping herself into the passenger seat, or as they referred to it, the "Command-Com" seat, next to her father.

"Pilot to co-pilot," Artemis said, as he always did before their trips. "All systems go?"

"Roger that, Captain," Curie said, sliding on her sunglasses. "All systems are A-OK. Kick the tires and light the fires!"

Artemis swung his sunglasses down over his prescription lenses and gave Curie the thumbs up, as he put the van into gear. "Mount St. Helens, here we come, ready or not."

Curie cranked up a tune on the radio. After the song ended, she turned to her father. "How was your visit with your old college friend?"

"Oh!" Artemis said. "We were more than just friends. We did everything together. We always said we wouldn't lose contact with each other, but our lives just got too busy." Artemis pushed his glasses further up on his nose.

"But to answer your question," Artemis said, "we had a great visit. It's always fun to reminisce over old times. The funny thing is that he has almost the exact itinerary as we do. He's on his way to Mount St. Helens right now, too..." Artemis paused. "Did we pack all of our instruments?"

"Yes, Dad we did," Curie said. "You were saying that he's on his way to Mount St. Helens?"

"I was?" Artemis said. "...Oh yes! I was, wasn't I."

"Sooo," Curie began, "where is he going after that?

"He's going to Hawaii in a few days for a marketing meeting for his high tech company," Artemis said. "In fact, he's staying at a hotel on the big island not far from us."

"Oh!" Curie said. "I thought he was another scientist."

Artemis laughed. "Bob, a scientist? No way!" he said. "We're going to see if we can hook up for dinner tomorrow night."

Curie felt something hit her in the back of her head. She turned and looked back at Nick. He had another balled-up piece of paper in his hand. He also had his forefinger over his lip, displaying the universal sign saying *be quiet*. He motioned for her to come back and sit next to him.

"I'll be back, Dad," Curie said, as she rushed back to Nick. Artemis automatically nodded a few times, deep in thought.

"What?" Curie asked.

"Don't you think it's a little **uncanny**," Nick asked, "that Dad runs into an old college roommate who just happens to be going everywhere we're going at the same time that we're being chased around by some maniacs?"

"When you put it that way," Curie said, "it does sound suspicious."

"The men aren't after us," Nick said. "They're after you."

"What!" Curie said. "What makes you think that?"

Nick told her what the man named Sheppard had said on the trail.

"But, why only me?" Curie asked.

Nick pointed to the key around her neck. "That's why," he said.

CHAPTER SEVEN:

Treason

Curie flipped open her laptop computer and started typing.

"What are you doing?" Nick asked, peering out the van window to see if they were being followed.

"I'm doing a search on Bob Connors," Curie said. "If he's got something to hide, I'll find it."

"Maybe he's a crook," Nick said. "Or just a big fake. Sometimes its hard to tell the two apart."

"Oh! Here you go!" Curie exclaimed. "Here's an article from earlier this year."

Bob   Connors   was released from county jail today after paying the half a million dollars needed to bail him out. Rumors of treason have surrounded Mr. Connors since the stories of his relationship with a former Russian spy, Katrina Kozlov, have surfaced.   Connors' position   with   Urban Aerospace Technologies, a supplier of military aircraft parts, allows him access to government secrets, which could be sold to our enemies.

"So, do you think he wants to steal HR?" Nick asked.

"No," Curie replied. "Like you said, they don't need me to steal HR. But they do need the key if they want to steal HR's motion computer chip."

"Okay," Nick said, "but even if they pry the key out of your steel-fisted grip, that only allows them to bypass the heat shield system. They still can't get access to the chip if they don't know the keypad code to open the power source bay inside."

"That's true," Curie said. "That is, unless they already know it!"

Little Gr
and Jumb
Shrimp

A small wisp of smoke drifted up from Mount St. Helens' horseshoe-shaped coned top. For the time being, the volcano was at peace.

"Boy," Nick said, standing on the observation deck at the Hoffstadt Bluffs Visitor Center, "if I thought Yellowstone was exciting, I was wrong. I mean, I know volcanoes rock, but this is nothing but a sleeping giant."

"I bet the people who live around here want it to remain a sleeping giant," Curie said. "Dad, isn't Mount St. Helens part of the Ring of Fire?"

Before Artemis could answer, Nick cut in. "Yes, it is," he said. "The Ring of Fire includes more than 160 volcanoes along the edge of the Pacific Ocean. More than half of the world's active volcanoes are in the ring." Nick scratched his head. "Although, I don't know why they call it that, because it's actually shaped like a horseshoe, just like the top of this volcano. But I guess the Horseshoe of Fire just doesn't have the right ring to it. No pun intended," Nick said with a chuckle.

"I'm so excited that HR can help volcanologists predict when volcanic eruptions will occur," Curie said.

"Besides that," Artemis added, "HR will give them a better sense of the massive forces involved in an explosive eruption. For example, the force of the Mount St. Helens eruption in 1980 was equal to 400 million tons of TNT!"

Artemis pointed to the valley below. "See that canyon down there?" he asked.

"The Little Grand Canyon," Curie said. "Yep, we're all set up for a tour of the canyon in an hour."

"Isn't that an oxymoron, Dad?" Nick asked.

"Isn't what an oxymoron?" Artemis said.

"Little GRAND canyon," Nick said.

Artemis laughed. "I hadn't thought of that, but yes, it is. I guess 'little grand' is kind of like 'jumbo shrimp,' just in reverse." Artemis paused for a few seconds trying to remember what he had been talking about.

"Oh, yes," Artemis continued. "That canyon was carved within one day by thick layers of mud from the volcano's eruption. The mixture then turned into hard rock that formed the stratified walls and cliffs of the canyon. A new fork of the Toutle River now flows through the canyon's floor."

RRRIIIINNNGGG!

Artemis' cell phone rang. He felt around in his pockets, moving his hands up and down frantically over his shirt and shorts pockets, but he couldn't find it.

"It's in the holster on your right hip, Dad," Curie said.

"Whew! Thanks," Artemis said, ripping it from the holster and flipping it open. "I always forget where I put this thing."

"Artemis," he said, speaking into the phone. "Bob, how are you?" Artemis listened for a few seconds to Bob. "Sure, we can meet you there. That's no problem. Okay, see you later."

Artemis turned toward his children. "Bob wants to buy us dinner at the hotel restaurant tonight," he said.

Curie saw Suni walking up to them. "Is Dr. Ki supposed to be here?" Curie asked. "I thought she went back to Hawaii."

"Artemis!" Suni said. "How are you?

Artemis turned. "Good morning! I thought you went home. To what do we owe this wonderful visit?"

"Artemis," Suni said, "I wish I could say this visit was for social reasons, but to be truthful, I came to pick you all up to head to Hawaii early. I just got reports that Mauna Loa may erupt soon, and we want to have you and HR on site as soon as possible."

"When will we be leaving?" Artemis asked.

"First thing in the morning," Suni replied. "But I have several other things I need to discuss with you. Have you had lunch yet?"

"Ahh," Artemis said, glancing at Curie and Nick. "We're scheduled to go on a hike through the Little Grand Canyon right now."

"This is really important," Suni said.

"Dad," Curie suggested, "why don't you and Dr. Ki go to lunch, and Nick and I will take the hike. Okay?"

Artemis hesitated for a few seconds. He really wanted to see the canyon, but a scientist's work is never done. "Okay, you guys be careful on your hike," Artemis said. "I'll meet you at the hotel after you're done. Let's keep in touch with our cell phones."

Suni turned and waved goodbye to Curie and Nick.

"I've got to get my hiking boots from the van," Nick said, smiling.

"What are you smiling about?" Curie asked. "We have to hike alone and then have dinner with the guy who may be trying to have me kidnapped."

"Hey!" Nick said. "A free dinner is a free dinner. Besides it would be kind of hard to kidnap you from the hotel restaurant. I'm feeling like a big hamburger, French fries, and a milkshake. What about you?"

"I guess you have a point," Curie agreed. "Just please stop talking about food with this long hike ahead of us! I'm craving some trail mix."

"Bird food!" Nick said with a smirk.

CHAPTER NINE

Too Smart for School!

Nick opened the back door of the van and grabbed his hiking boots. Almost every square inch of the rear bumper and a good portion of the back doors were covered in bumper stickers. Nick's favorite one was the neon green sticker stuck between Ohio and North Dakota on the bottom of the left door. It read: MY KIDS ARE TOO SMART FOR SCHOOL!

Nick noticed that one of the 'O's' in 'SCHOOL' was filled with a glob of mud. He was about to swipe it off when he realized that it wasn't mud. He plucked off a round magnetic device and rolled it between his fingers.

"Are you ready to go?" Curie said. "The hike starts in 15 minutes."

Nick dropped the device into his soft drink cup. He walked over to a trashcan, gently set the cup into it, and motioned for his sister to follow him.

"What was that?" Curie asked.

"It was a listening device," Nick said. "They could hear everything we were saying when we were inside the van!"

"Are you sure it wasn't a tracking device?" Curie asked.

"Yep," Nick replied. "Dad and I looked at similar ones a few months ago for another project."

"But," Curie's voice was slightly frantic, "that means they know everything, including the power source access code."

"What!" Nick exclaimed. "How would they know that?" Then he remembered— Curie told him the code when he had forgotten it the other day.

"Oh man, I'm sorry," Nick said. "That means all they need is the key. That's why they're after you, for sure."

"You sure know how to make a girl feel safe," Curie said. "Come on, we've got to meet up with the other hikers."

"Don't you think we should tell Dad?" Nick said.

"Not until we know who's behind this," Curie said.

CHAPTER TEN:

Taking Care of Business

The group of hikers rounded a bend, and the guide stopped. "See these striations?" he said. "Until this canyon was formed after the eruption, scientists believed it took years for each of these striated segments to form. Now, because of this canyon, many scientists are rethinking that presupposition."

A young red-haired boy at the front of the group raised his hand. "What's a presupposition?" he asked.

"It's when you believe that something is true before you have any proof that it is," the guide said.

Curie and Nick lagged at the back of the group. Curie turned to tell Nick something, but he wasn't there! Instead, he was waving to her from a small cave beyond some boulders. When the guide wasn't looking, she ran over to join him.

"What in the world are you doing?" Curie asked.

"I think we're being followed," Nick said. "Quick, hide in here."

Curie and Nick had just ducked behind a large boulder near the cave when Sheppard and McGee came around the bend. Curie watched fearfully as the tour group moved on, unknowingly leaving them behind.

The men stopped to rest. "This is ridiculous!" McGee said, taking his suit coat off and wiping sweat from his brow with the back of his hand. "We can't just go up and drag her out of the group. We'd be better off trying to grab her at the hotel."

"For once, I have to agree with you," Sheppard said, running his hand over his beard. "But if we don't get her today, the boss is going to be very upset. You know how she gets when things don't go as planned. The bidders are in place, just waiting for us to get to Hawaii. We need that key so we can open that stupid robot. The highest bidder gets the merchandise, and we get rich!"

"Then we need to get the girl quickly," McGee said. "Let's get back to the hotel."

Nick's knee was starting to hurt from its awkward position. He shifted it just a little, but in the process, loosened some gravel that skipped down the trail toward the men.

"What was that?" McGee asked.

Sheppard took a few steps forward, when suddenly a small chipmunk ran out from between two boulders.

The two men laughed. "I'll be glad when we're done with this," Sheppard said.

Curie and Nick waited, motionless, for several minutes before scrambling out from behind the boulder.

"Did you hear that?" Curie said. "They're going to sell the motion computer chip to the highest bidder. We can't let that happen!"

"You're right, big sister," Nick said.

"We need to call the police, the FBI, and the CIA," Curie almost shouted.

"No!" Nick said. "They won't believe two kids without any proof. So, we're going to have to get them caught by ourselves. Then we have to find their leader, because unless Bob is a woman disguised as a man, it's not him!"

"What do you mean by 'get them caught'?" Curie asked.

"Let's just say that I have a plan!" Nick said, as a wry smile appeared on his face. "But first, we need to go back to the van."

Curie shook her head, very unsure whether they were doing the right thing.

CHAPTER ELEVEN:

Keep Your Hands Off My Gold

Nick and Curie snuck into the hotel through a back entrance. They tiptoed toward the lobby where they saw Sheppard and McGee trying to blend in with the other hotel guests. Most of them were there for the day attending a coin collector's exhibition in the grand ballroom. Two hotel policemen stood by the front door.

"Curie, see that garden area with all the big palm plants?" Nick asked.

Curie nodded. "Do you really think this is going to work?"

"I've seen it work on a TV show, so there's only one way to find out," Nick said. "Are you ready?

Curie nodded.

"Okay," Nick said. "I'll give you a minute to get into position, and then I'll set up the targets. They're both wearing suit coats, just like they were earlier, so you shouldn't have any problem accomplishing your part of the mission. But wait until I get them to reach out before making the drop. That way, their suit coat pockets will be away from their bodies and they won't feel anything."

Curie nodded again, took a deep breath and was off. She dashed between and around columns and planters, while watching where the men were looking. Finally she reached the back of the garden. When no one was looking her way, she stepped into the garden and buried herself within the broad, thick leaves. She slithered forward, but made sure she was still well hidden. She removed two objects from her pocket and waited with one object in each hand.

Nick saw that she was in place to execute his plan. He sauntered out where the men could see him clearly. McGee spied him first and alerted Sheppard. They rushed over to him.

"You, Nick," Sheppard ordered. "Stop right where you are!"

Nick took one more step and stopped right in front of Curie. "Hey, fellas," Nick said, putting his hands up, palms out, in a "wait a minute" gesture.

"I thought you two were bear meat," Nick said, as he backed up in a semi-circle. The men moved slowly after him. Nick stopped when they were positioned in front of Curie. He could see her sliding forward quietly. "How did you escape that bear?" he asked.

"We made it down to..." McGee started to say until Sheppard hit him on the arm.

"That's not important," Sheppard said. "What is important is your sister. Where is she?"

Nick rubbed his chin with his hand. "Oh, so that's why you were chasing us," he said. "What's so important about my sister? I'm the smarter one." Nick saw Curie stick her tongue out at him.

They were about 15 paces from the front desk. Nick saw one of the hotel policemen walking toward the desk.

"You can come with us until we get her," Sheppard said.

"I'll tell you what," Nick said. "Why don't I just scream for help from that policeman instead?" Nick started to open his mouth as if he were going to scream.

Both men shoved their arms up in the air to try to grab him so he wouldn't shout.

"No! No!" they both said.

Curie swiftly dropped the objects into the side pockets of their suit coats. McGee's left arm came down quickly. As Curie pulled her hand back, her fingers brushed his coat sleeve. She ducked back into the palm garden, just as McGee turned to look behind him.

"Listen, kid," Sheppard said. "If you don't come with us and help us get your sister, we'll find your father and..."

"HELP! HELP ME!" Nick screamed. As the two men turned to run, Curie, who had come out from the garden, knocked over a mop bucket, and water gushed across the floor in front of them.

WHOOOAAAAAAA!!

Sheppard and McGee screeched as they slid wildly across the lobby, crashing in front of the policemen by the front door.

The two police officers grabbed the men as Nick slid on the water toward them like he was on a skateboard. "What did these guys do, kid?" one of the policemen asked.

"I saw them hurrying out of the ballroom," Nick said, pointing at the ballroom entrance where a big banner said, *Coin Collector's Exhibit.* "I heard that some coins were stolen from someone in there. I think you should check these guys!"

"That's ridiculous, officer," Sheppard said. "We're not thieves."

"Can you prove they took the coins, kid?" the policeman asked.

"No," Nick admitted, "but I saw the look on their faces, and I can hear jingling in their pockets."

"Let's just check and see," one of the officers said. Each of the officers reached into the men's pockets and pulled out a gold coin. The crowd forming around them included Artemis and Suni, who pushed their way forward to get to Nick.

"See, I told you," Nick said to the officers. "These guys are crooks."

"We didn't steal those coins," Sheppard protested.

Nick saw his dad and Suni come through the crowd. Suni had her eye on the bearded man named Sheppard. The look on Sheppard's face, as he looked back at Suni, was not only one of recognition, but also that of an employee being scolded by his boss.

Nick suddenly realized that Sheppard worked for Suni, and not for Bob Connors!

CHAPTER TWELVE:

Circumstantial Evidence

The evening sun had set brilliantly on the horizon as Artemis drove toward Seattle where they were to catch their morning flight to Hawaii. When the last edge of the sun sank behind the distant clouds, Curie turned to her father. "How long do you think those men will be in jail?" she asked.

Artemis was lost in thought.

"Dad!" Curie said, tapping him on the arm.

"I'm sorry," Artemis said. "Did you say something?"

"Yes," Curie replied. "I was wondering if you had any idea how long those men would be in jail."

"Oh!" Artemis said. "Since it's Friday, they probably won't see a judge until Monday morning. Then they can get out on bail if they have the money."

Curie gazed back at Nick, and they each smiled.

"Will you be okay if I go back by Nick?" Curie asked.

"Sure," Artemis said. "We'll be in Seattle in an hour."

Curie sat next to her brother. "We've got a couple of days to find the person behind this before those goons get out of jail," she said.

"We don't need a couple of days," Nick said. "I already know who's behind it, and you won't be happy with who it is."

"You do?" Curie said. "Who is it?"

"Dr. Suni Ki," Nick replied.

"No way," Curie said. "She's too nice."

"Maybe she appears to be," Nick said, "but she's the one behind this. Remember how Dad told us that sometimes the nicest people turn out to be the worst people? Suni's a professional thief."

"So, what are we going to do?" Curie said. "The word of two kids against a famous volcanologist isn't going to get us anywhere."

"That's for sure," Nick said. "We have to get some sort of proof and also figure a way to trap her to prove she's guilty. What can you find on her on the Internet?"

Curie's hands flew over her keyboard. A long list of accomplishments came up on the screen. "Nothing out of the ordinary," Curie sighed. "After getting her doctorate degree, she worked for several corporate groups involved in volcano research and possible use of volcano resources. Two were American, and one was Indonesian."

"Open that article," Nick said, pointing to one that said,

Top   volcanologist   slightly injured in robbery.

They both scanned the article, reading that Suni had been slightly injured in a robbery at a high-tech company in Indonesia. The robbery did not take place where she worked, but while she was visiting her boyfriend at his job.

"Huh!" Nick said. "I bet she was behind the robbery."

"Oh!" Curie said. "That gives me an idea." Curie searched for other high-tech robberies in Indonesia during the three years Suni lived there.

"According to this," Curie said, "there were six corporate robberies of American interests while Suni lived in Indonesia. Let me pull up some images of the robberies."

They scanned through the photos and saw Suni at the same time. In one photo, a crowd was visible in the background of the picture. Suni's face was in the middle of the crowd.

"This is a picture of the first robbery at Whist Technologies six months after she arrived in Indonesia. That puts her at two of the robberies," Nick said. "That can't just be a coincidence. But it's still not real evidence, either."

"Hold it!" Curie said, as she copied the photograph and opened a special graphics enhancement program the government had given them to use on a project last year. When the program came up, Curie pasted the photo into it and clicked an icon that read, *Wash Clean*. The picture disappeared and slowly began to rebuild itself from the bottom up.

After it was done, they looked at it again. "There's our evidence!" Curie said. "And it's real evidence."

"What are you talking about?" Nick asked. "I don't see anything different, except that it's just sharper, and Suni has a smirk on her face."

Curie zoomed in on a section of the photograph below Suni's head and between the two people in front of her. As the picture came into focus, Nick saw what Curie had seen already. Hanging from Suni's shirt collar was an employee ID with the words *Whist Tech* over her photo. Below her photo, it read, *Computer Analyst.*

Curie and Nick both knew that Suni hated computers. Or, she said she did!

CHAPTER THIRTEEN:

A Scientist . . . or a Detective

After a good night's sleep and a short conversation, while their dad was taking a shower, Curie and Nick decided they had to let him in on what they knew so far.

"Dad," Curie said, "Nick and I need to talk with you before we head to the airport."

Artemis looked at his watch. "We have time," he said. "What's up? Something's wrong. I can tell by the tone of your voice."

"We didn't tell you everything about the bear," Curie said. She told Artemis what had really happened and all about what they had overheard in the Little Grand Canyon.

"You mean those two men at the hotel were trying to kidnap you to get the key?" Artemis asked in disbelief. He was visibly upset.

"Yep!" Nick said. "That's why we had to do something. We didn't want to be looking over our shoulders everywhere we went. So we planted the gold coins on them so the police would investigate them and keep them away from us for a while."

"My, my," Artemis said, as a slight smile appeared on his face. "You have been busy working on this mystery."

"Last night, we figured out who's behind the plot to steal HR's motion computer chip, and you're not going to believe it," Curie said. "At first we thought it was your friend, Bob."

"Bob would never be involved in anything like this," Artemis said.

"Yeah," Nick said. "We finally figured out we had the wrong person."

Curie handed her father the evidence they printed out yesterday.

Artemis examined the picture and the other printouts. "You guys really used your brains on this one," he said. "Being a scientist is like being a detective. You dig up evidence and draw conclusions from that evidence. You both are well on your way to being full-fledged scientists, but you've definitely shown you would make great detectives, too!"

"I have to apologize to you, Curie," Artemis said. "I was supposed to take that key. But I got so excited about going sightseeing at Yellowstone that I forgot to grab it before leaving the van." Artemis pointed to the key in Curie's hand. "I never meant to put you kids in danger."

"What are you talking about, Dad?" Curie said, handing the key to her father.

"A few weeks ago," Artemis explained, "agents from the FBI approached me about Suni's previous activities. I was supposed to be the bait, not you." Artemis pulled out a cigarette lighter from his pocket.

"This is a tracking device and a miniature recorder, and the lighter really works, too," he said. He flicked the switch, and the lighter's flame shot into the air. "FBI agents have been tracking me since we put the chip into HR."

"Our dad is an undercover agent for the government," Nick said. "How cool is that?"

"Yeah," Artemis said, "but I'm not a very good agent. I let the key out of my sight and almost got Curie kidnapped. I'm no James Bond, that's for sure."

Curie hugged her dad. "We don't want James Bond as a father. We want a wild and crazy scientist," she said.

"Yeah, Dad," Nick said. "You're cool the way you are."

"Thanks, kids," Artemis said. "But we still have to get the goods on Suni."

"Won't that evidence help?" Curie asked.

"Nope," Artemis said. "This is the exact stuff the FBI showed me. That's why I said you guys could be detectives, because you discovered the exact same evidence they uncovered about Suni."

"Well then," Nick said. "It's time for the Masters of Disasters to come to the rescue. We need a plan, and here's what I think we should do..."

CHAPTER FOURTEEN

A Momentous Occasion

Curie sat at her laptop in a building just two miles from Mauna Loa's summit. A huge picture window in front of her framed a breathtaking view of the smoldering volcano.

She was fascinated by Hawaii's volcanoes because she had read they didn't erupt violently. They just overflowed. You could stand a few feet away from the lava, or as close as you could withstand the intense heat, and watch the lava ooze slowly across the ground.

"Dad," Nick said. "HR's systems are A-OK."

"That's great!" Artemis shouted, sitting at a computer which provided him with the latest GPS, tilt, and seismic readings on Mauna Loa's internal activities.

"Kids, this thing's getting ready to erupt!" Artemis said. "The most recent GPS is showing that the crater dome has increased over the last 24 hours by 40 percent. The tiltmeters on the southwest side, which show how much the ground is tilting due to the expansion of the dome, are off the chart and..."

The ground began to shake beneath their feet. Curie grabbed her computer to make sure it didn't vibrate off the table. Nick clung to HR to keep him from tipping over.

After everything settled down, Artemis stared at the computer monitor. "That was a 6.6," Artemis said. "The quakes have been coming two to three times an hour, and they're increasing in intensity. This is a momentous occasion! Mauna Loa hasn't erupted since 1984. You guys are in for a treat."

"Great, Dad," Nick said. "There's nothing as fun as sitting on top of a volcano that's about to overflow with molten rock that can burn a hole right through you in a matter of seconds."

The door opened, and Suni walked in, her heels clicking on the shiny wood floor.

Artemis was still concentrating on the volcano's activity. "The quakes are getting more intense," he remarked. "It won't be long. We have to get HR down into the steam vent at Mauna Loa's southeast rift zone."

"Not quite," Suni said. Artemis' head snapped up as Sheppard and McGee entered the room. "Curie, I've got to admit you're a hard girl to corner."

Suni stared at the panel access key around Curie's neck. "Curie and Nick, let me formally introduce you to Sheppard and McGee, although you have met before," she said. "Artemis, unlike you, your children are very clever."

"I've always said that," Artemis said.

Suni thrust her hand toward Curie. "Give me the key!" she said.

Curie quickly removed the chain around her neck and handed it to Suni.

"You don't have to do this, Suni!" Artemis asked. "Whatever you're after isn't worth it."

"I want the motion computer chip you designed," Suni said. "I've got buyers ready to take it to the next step."

"What do you mean, the next step?" Artemis said, surprised.

"You're so naïve, Artemis," Suni said. "You don't even know when you've created something of immense value. Your chip is the miracle that scientists in the field of advanced bionics have been waiting for."

"Bionics?" Artemis said.

"You mean, like in the 'Bionic Woman'?" Nick asked.

"See?" Suni said. "Nick's way ahead of you again. Yes! Your chip can control bionic limbs attached to amputees, or people who have lost their arms and legs. How much do you think they'll pay to have the use of their hands or legs back? Soon quadriplegics, who can't move their bodies below their necks, will be moving around of their own free will. Your chip is priceless. Well, not exactly. I have a very specific price in mind," Suni added, with a haughty laugh.

"To think that people believe you're a genius," Suni said. "They're wrong, or you would have figured all of this out for yourself."

Artemis smiled. "It's funny you should say that," he said. "Because, just this morning I took Curie and Nick's advice and completed the donation of the rights to the design of my..." Artemis looked at Curie and Nick, "...*our* motion computer chip to the Amputee Coalition of America."

"What???" Suni asked in dismay.

"You are right about me being naïve, though," Artemis said. "I never for a minute thought that someone would want to gain monetarily from something that could help so many people. I'm sure the FBI will understand someone like you better than I can."

"FBI!" Suni said.

Just then, agents appeared from behind the curtains. The door burst open and several more agents poured into the room.

"So my friend, who's the genius now?"
Artemis asked.

CHAPTER FIFTEEN:

Dad's Donation

HR moved gracefully down into the steam vent until he was out of sight. The readings he was sending back were extraordinary. HR was working better than Artemis had hoped.

"So, when you donated the chip design, what did they say?" Nick asked.

"They were overjoyed," Artemis said. "They couldn't understand why I didn't want to sell the design to some technology corporation for a large sum of money."

"What did you tell them?" Curie asked.

"I told them that it was my children who had the idea of donating the chip, and that I was very proud of them," Artemis replied. "I also told them that all the money in the world couldn't buy what I hold dearest. You two never cease to amaze me."

"Dad," Curie said, "that's because we take after you!"

The ground suddenly shook, and the sky at the southwest corner of the volcano glowed a brilliant reddish-orange as lava poured out of the cone.

"Dad," Nick remarked, gazing at the unforgettable sight, "right now, I wouldn't want to be anywhere but sitting on top of a volcano that's spewing lava, with you and Curie by my side."

THE END

ABOUT THE AUTHOR

Carole Marsh is an author and publisher who has written many works of fiction and non-fiction for young readers. She travels throughout the United States and around the world to research her books. In 1979 Carole Marsh was named Communicator of the Year for her corporate communications work with major national and international corporations.

Marsh is the founder and CEO of Gallopade International, established in 1979. Today, Gallopade International is widely recognized as a leading source of educational materials for every state and many countries. Marsh and Gallopade were recipients of the 2004 Teachers' Choice Award. Marsh has written more than 50 Carole Marsh Mysteries™. In 2007, she was named Georgia Author of the Year. Years ago, her children, Michele and Michael, were the original characters in her mystery books. Today, they continue the Carole Marsh Books tradition by working at Gallopade. By adding grandchildren Grant and Christina as new mystery characters, she has continued the tradition for a third generation.

Ms. Marsh welcomes correspondence from her readers. You can e-mail her at fanclub@gallopade.com, visit carolemarshmysteries.com, or write to her in care of Gallopade International, P.O. Box 2779, Peachtree City, Georgia, 30269 USA.

Book Club
Talk About It!

1. Have you ever seen a volcano? Would you
   like to visit one? Why or why not?

2. Are you more like Nick or Curie? Explain
   why.

3. What was your favorite part of the book?
   Why? Was it exciting, scary, or happy?

4. Artemis meets his old college friend, Bob
   Conners, at Yellowstone National Park. He
   tells Nick and Curie that sometimes you lose
   track of your friends even when you don't
   mean to. Have you ever lost track of a good
   friend? What can you do to keep in touch
   with friends you have now?

5. Artemis gave the rights to his invention to
   the Amputee Coalition of America. Do you
   think that was the right thing to do? Why or
   why not?

6. Nick and Curie catch the thieves at a coin
   collectors' convention. Do you like to

collect anything like coins, stamps, dolls, or
baseball cards?   If so, talk about why you
collect that certain thing. Why did you
start? How many do you have? What's your
favorite?

7. Nick and Curie couldn't prove that Suni Ki
was a thief until they found "substantial
evidence." Do you think saying someone
did something wrong is enough, or should
you have to prove they did something
wrong?

8. The kids put fake coins into the thieves'
pockets because the same move worked
once in a movie they had seen. Do you
think things from movies can work in real
life? Why should you be careful about
trying movie stunts?

9. Nick and Curie decided not to tell their
father about the listening device on their
van because they wanted to know more
before they went to him. Do you think they
did the right thing? Why or why not?

Book Club
Bring It to Life!

1. It's the same difference, right? Have each member of the group come up with as many oxymorons as they can. Nick and Curie already came up with Little Grand Canyon and jumbo shrimp. See what you can think of! If you get stuck, ask a member's parents for some help.

2. Make your own robot! Have each member find a square cardboard box. Cover the box in aluminum foil. Then find things around the house like buttons, paper clips, or shiny ribbon. Decorate the box to look like your very own robot. Does it talk? What does it do?

3. What would you say? Create your own bumper stickers like Nick and Curie have on the back of their van. Come up with funny phrases and write them on rectangular pieces of paper. Then, use tape to attach the homemade bumper stickers to a special notebook—maybe the one you use for Book Club.

4. Nick and Curie used the Internet to help them find information to solve the mystery. You can be a detective, too! Have each member pick one thing about volcanoes that interests them (it could be eruptions, lava, ash...whatever). Then, have each member research that topic using google.com, yahoo.com, or ask.com, and present a short report to the group. Be sure to ask lots of questions to learn as much as you can!

GLOSSARY

extraterrestrial: a being that is not from this earth

obstacle: something that stands in the way of someone's progress

phonetic: spelling a word the way it sounds

 precarious: not secure or dangerous

quadriplegic: a person who is paralyzed in both arms and legs

reminisce: to fondly recall the past

striated: marked with lines or grooves

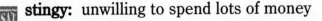 **stingy:** unwilling to spend lots of money

turbulent: when something is bumpy or in disorder

 uncanny: something that is supernatural or mysterious

 validate: to make official

 zealous: to be full of enthusiasm or eager to do something

VOLCANO Scavenger Hunt

Want to have some fun? Let's go on a scavenger hunt! Find the items below related to the mystery. *(Teachers: you have permission to reproduce this page for your students.)*

_____ 1. a key

_____ 2. a picture of a laptop computer

_____ 3. a picture of a volcano

_____ 4. a stuffed teddy bear (just as cute as the bear Nick and Curie see at Yellowstone!)

_____ 5. an ID badge like people wear at a government facility

_____ 6. a pair of glasses (like that crazy scientist, Artemis!)

_____ 7. a man's suit jacket

_____ 8. a white shirt with buttons down the front (just like a scientist's coat!)

_____ 9. a pair of hiking boots

_____ 10. a couple of coins

VOLCANO POP QUIZ

1. What does HR stand for?

2. Where do Nick and Curie first test HR?

3. True or False? Yellowstone is considered to be a supervolcano.

4. What did the men want to steal from Curie?

5. What was HR's code?

6. Why did Suni Ki want to steal HR?

7. In what year did Mount St. Helens last erupt?

8. What kind of convention was going on at the hotel?

VOLCANO Trivia

1. There are more than 1,500 active volcanoes in the world.

2. Crater Lake in Oregon was formed when a volcano lost its top in an eruption thousands of years ago.

3. Volcanoes erupt in different ways. Sometimes the eruption is quiet with slow-moving lava, and sometimes it's a big explosion of lava and ash.

4. Fresh ash (which is pulverized rock) from a volcanic eruption can be acidic and smelly!

5. Hawaii was formed by hundreds of underwater volcanoes that erupted thousands of years ago.

Hawaii

6. A dormant volcano is one that has not erupted in many years, but may still erupt at any time.

7. Mauna Loa is the world's largest active volcano. It is taller than Mount Everest!

8. People like to live on the slopes of inactive volcanoes because the soil there is fertile (that means it's good for growing a garden).

9. Indonesia is the country with the most volcanoes in the world! There is a volcano almost everywhere you look!

10. While there are about 1,500 active volcanoes on land, there are an estimated 10,000 volcanoes in the ocean! That's a lot of wet lava!

11. While you are reading this, 20 volcanoes are erupting worldwide!

12. The tallest known volcano is Olympus Mons on the planet Mars.

13. Italy's Stromboli volcano has been erupting for the last 2,500 years.

14. Three days after the 1980 eruption of Mount St. Helens, ash had traveled across the entire United States.

15. The 1883 eruption of Indonesia's Krakatoa volcano produced a blast heard 3,000 miles away.

Yellowstone National Park Trivia

1. Nearly 4,000 bison, also known as buffalo, live in Yellowstone.
2. There are more thermal features in Yellowstone than any other place on earth, like geysers, hot springs and steam vents.
3. After Congress saw photographs and paintings of Yellowstone, they decided to make it the first national park to protect it for everyone to enjoy.
4. When hiking in Yellowstone, you should make noise so you don't surprise any bears!
5. The center of Yellowstone Park sits on a large volcano that has been dormant for 600,000 years.
6. Steamboat Geyser in Yellowstone National Park is the highest erupting geyser in the world.
7. Yellowstone's isolated southwest corner is famous for dozens of waterfalls.
8. Yellowstone National Park is located in Wyoming, Montana, and Idaho.

TECH CONNECTS

Hey, Kids!
Visit www.carolemarshmysteries.com to:

Join the Carole Marsh Mysteries Fan Club!

Write one sensational sentence using all five SAT words in the glossary!

Download a Volcano Word Search!

Take a Pop Quiz!

Download a Scavenger Hunt!

Read Voracious Volcano Trivia!

Read Yellowstone National Park Trivia!